Dial Books for Young Readers

New York

December's Travels

by MISCHA DAMJAN

pictures by DUŠAN KÁLLAY

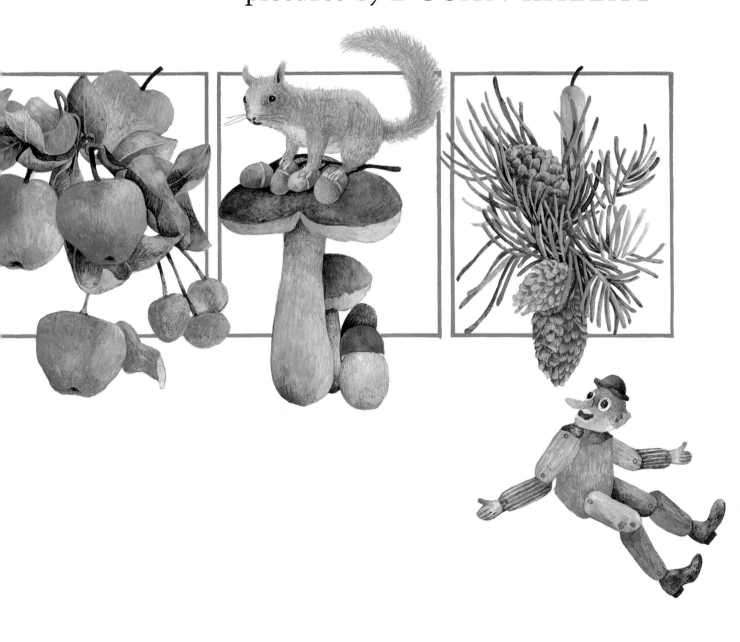

Dec ecember lived alone,
far away in a cold northern land.
For eleven months of the year
December slept, but in his own
month he was always busy. He
called the wind to sweep the last
leaves from the trees. He had the
lights lit because the days were so
short. He sent showers of snow over
the countryside to cover up the
grass on frosty winter days.

December never thought about his life until one stormy night when the North Wind came to visit. He told December stories about the other months of the year—about the promise of spring and the bright fields of summer and about the autumn harvest.

It was getting close to Christmas and December had many toys and kites to make, but after the North Wind's visit he felt strangely sad and restless. He wondered what the other months were like and wished that he could meet them.

The days in December's own month were passing quickly. As soon as the church bells rang in the new year, December's time would be up. He would have to go to sleep for another eleven months, never to wake up until the earth was cold and the trees were bare again.

Just before midnight on the last day of the year, the North Wind knocked at December's window. "I've been thinking about you, my friend," he said gaily. "As a New Year's present I shall send you to visit some of the other months— March and June and October, I think."

Then, without another word, the North Wind blew away. December suddenly felt very tired so he lay down under his covers and closed his eyes.

The next thing he knew, he was standing by a hillside on a clear blue day. The West Wind was driving the snow from the valleys and a thrush was building its nest.

December suddenly realized that a boy was standing next to him. "I am March," the boy said. "And who are you?"

"My name is December. It's very beautiful here. Will you show me around?"

"Happily," said March. He took December's arm and the two set off. But hardly had they started to cross the fields when dark clouds came up from the horizon and thousands of snowflakes blocked the sun.

"I'm very moody, you know," said March, winking.

At that very moment December thought he heard a lark singing joyfully in the swirling storm.

During the next few days as March and December became friends, the sun grew stronger and stronger. The swallows came back from the south, and one of them brought news that the storks and cranes were on their way as well.

"Winter cannot last!" March cried. "Now it is my best time."

On the last day of his month
March took December to a country
fair. Never before had December
seen such wonders! There was a
strongman who could tear chains
with his bare hands and there was
a man who ate fire; there were
clowns galore and musicians
playing flutes.

But as it grew close to midnight,
the calliope stopped tinkling, the
crowd disappeared, and the clowns
went home to sleep. Now December
and March were alone on the
midway.

"Good-bye, good-bye, my dear
friend," said March. "Remember
my fickle winds and flocks of birds
in your own time."

December made this promise.
Then he lay next to a circus van
and fell asleep.

When December awoke, he was sitting beneath a blooming chestnut tree. As he was admiring its colors, a boy wearing a hat made of flowers sat down. "I am June," said the boy. "And you must be December. Lovely day, don't you agree?"

December thought there were no words to describe it. The entire countryside seemed composed of sky and meadows, flowers, butterflies, and fluttering birds.

Then June and December ran to the hills where sheep were grazing. They danced to the shepherd's pipes and played with the little lambs until the sun went down.

"Cuckoo! Cuckoo! Cuckoo!" the cuckoo bird cried. The newly mown meadows slumbered but the scythes had left a faint ringing in the air.

Late that evening June and December heard a delicate chirping song. "What is that?" asked December.

"A cricket," said June. "You mean you've never heard a cricket?"

Then a raucous croaking came from the ponds. "And what is that?" asked December.

"Frogs!" said June. "Why, you hardly know anything!"

As the long summer days went by, June and December became fast friends. They searched for crickets and frogs, and climbed trees to admire the fragile eggs in their nests.

On the last day of the month there was a thunderstorm at midnight. The time had come to say good-bye. "Promise me you will remember our green and golden days together," June said to December.

"I will always remember," said December.

Then he lay down beneath the sheltering branches of the chestnut tree where he'd first met June. Soon he was fast asleep.

When December awoke, it was a mild sunny day. But the shadows had lengthened and the grass in the meadows was brittle.

December was examining a full, heavy sunflower when a boy came along wearing clothes of bright yellow and a hat shaped like an apple. "I am October," said the boy.

"My name is December and I'm very glad to meet you," said December.

Then the two walked together through the orchards and picked the fruit from the trees.

With the first autumn winds the swallows returned south;
soon the storks and the cuckoo were gone as well. Only the crows
were left, sitting black and silent on the half-bare branches.

December looked at his friend and thought that he seemed sad.
"Let me make you a kite," he said. Quickly he fashioned one,
drawing a bird with bright plumage to comfort October.

The boy's face glowed with pleasure as he took the string and
flew the kite higher and higher.

It rarely rained and the sunsets were beautiful, but each day
was shorter and colder than the last. Finally the shepherds herded
the sheep and rams down from the mountainsides to the warm,
sheltering barns. October's time was coming to an end.

"Good-bye, my friend," he said to December on the very last
night at midnight. "Remember my lingering beauty and make
the coldness of your own time shine with light."

"I will try," said December. Then he lay down to sleep beneath
the twinkling stars.

When he awoke, December was back in his own land. The hills were gray and empty, and the air was electric with cold.

He thought of his friends, of March and June and October, and suddenly for the first time he was lonely. After considering the matter, December set to work making mangers for the beasts and feeding tables for the birds so that they might come close to him when the snows began. Then he left his mountaintop and went down into the valleys to make new friends.

Those he met were willing and warm, and together they collected apples and pears, honey and nuts and cheeses—food from the year's harvest. The children helped in the kitchens, baking cakes and pretzels to give at Christmas.

On each day of his month December ventured farther and farther into the world. Along the way more and more friends joined him, bearing gifts. By Christmas they were a multitude.

The snows had come by now, turning the countryside white. But when December looked closely at the snowflakes they sparkled with all the colors of the rainbow. He didn't feel the cold, surrounded as he was by new friends and memories of old ones.

The North Wind did not come again to visit, but December was content. He knew that though he might sleep the next eleven months away, his dreams would be full of wonder. March and June and October would be there, vivid and real, and in this way he would keep them with him always.

First published in the United States by
Dial Books for Young Readers
2 Park Avenue / New York, New York 10016

Published simultaneously in Canada by Fitzhenry & Whiteside Limited, Toronto
Published in West Germany by Otto Maier Verlag as *Dezember und seine Freunde*
Copyright ©1986 by Otto Maier Verlag Ravensburg / Translated by Anthea Bell
Layout by L'Ubomir Krátky Bratislava / Typography by Jane Byers Bierhorst
This adaptation copyright ©1986 by Dial Books for Young Readers / All rights reserved
Printed in Germany / First edition
COBE
10 9 8 7 6 5 4 3 2 1

Library of Congress Cataloging-in-Publication Data

Damjan, Mischa, pseud. / December's Travels

Translation of / Dezember und seine Freunde.
Summary / The boy December isn't as enthusiastic about readying his month
this year until a trip to some of the other months makes him appreciate his own.
[1. Months—Fiction. 2. Christmas—Fiction.]   I. Kállay, Dušan, ill. II. Title.
PZ7.D185De 1986   [E]   86-2155
ISBN 0-8037-0257-4

The artwork for each picture consists of an ink, watercolor, and acrylic
painting, which is camera-separated and reproduced in full color.

To
my
son
Mischa
M. D.